The Adventures of
JOHNNY CHUCK

The Adventures of

JOHNNY CHUCK

by Thornton W. Burgess
illustrated by Harrison Cady

**tempo
books**

GROSSET & DUNLAP
A FILMWAYS COMPANY
Publishers • New York

Contents

[v]

CONTENTS

Illustrations

[*vii*]

ILLUSTRATIONS

I

Gentle Sister South Wind Arrives

"Good news, good news for everyone, above or
down below,
For Master Winsome Bluebird's come to whistle
off the snow!"

ALL THE GREEN MEADOWS and all the Green Forest had heard the news. Peter Rabbit had seen to that. And just as soon as each of the little meadow and forest folks heard it, he hurried out to listen for himself and make sure that it was true. And each, when he heard that sweet voice of Winsome Bluebird, had kicked up his heels and shouted "Hurrah!"

You see, they all knew that Winsome Bluebird never is very far ahead of gentle Sister South Wind, and that when she arrives, blustering, rough Brother North Wind is already on his way back to the cold, cold land where the ice never melts.

Of course Winsome Bluebird doesn't really whistle off the snow, but after he comes, the snow disappears so fast that it seems as if he did. It is surprising what a difference a little good news makes. Of course nothing had really changed that first day when Winsome Bluebird's whistle was heard on the Green Meadows and in the Green Forest, but it seemed as if everything had changed. And it was all because that sweet whistle was a promise, a promise that everyone knew would come true. And so there was joy in all the hearts on the Green Meadows and in the Green Forest. Even grim old Granny Fox felt it, and as for Reddy Fox, why, Reddy even shouted good-naturedly to Peter Rabbit and hoped he was feeling well.

And then gentle Sister South

Wind arrived. She came in the night, and in the morning there she was, hard at work making the Green Meadows and the Green Forest ready for Mistress Spring. She broke the icy bands that had bound the Smiling Pool and the Laughing Brook so long; and the Smiling Pool began to smile once more, and the Laughing Brook to gurgle and then to laugh and finally to sing merrily.

She touched the little banks of snow that remained, and straightway they melted and disappeared. She kissed the eight babies of Unc' Billy Possum, and they kicked off the bedclothes under which old Mrs. Possum had tucked them and scrambled out of the big hollow tree to play.

She peeped in at the door of Johnny Chuck and called softly, and Johnny Chuck awoke from his long sleep and yawned and began to think about getting up. She knocked at the door of Digger the Badger, and Digger awoke. She tickled the nose of Striped Chipmunk, who was about half awake, and Striped Chipmunk sneezed and then he hopped out of bed and hurried up to his doorway to shout good morning after her, as she hurried over to see if Bobby Coon was still sleeping.

Peter Rabbit followed her

Peter Rabbit followed her about

about. He couldn't understand it
at all. Peter had smiled to himself when he heard how softly
she had called at the doorway of
Johnny Chuck's house, for many
and many a time during the
long winter Peter had stopped
at Johnny Chuck's house and
shouted down the long hall at
the top of his voice without once
waking Johnny Chuck. Now Peter
nearly tumbled over with surprise, as he heard Johnny Chuck
yawn at the first low call of
gentle Sister South Wind.

"How does she do it? I don't
understand it at all," said Peter,
as he scratched his long left ear
with his long left hind leg.

Gentle Sister South Wind smiled at Peter. "There are a lot of things in this world that you will never understand, Peter Rabbit. You will just have to believe them without understanding them and be content to know that they are so," she said, and hurried over to the Green Forest to tell Unc' Billy Possum that his old friend, Ol' Mistah Buzzard, was on his way up from ol' Virginny.

II

Johnny Chuck
Receives Callers

THE MORNING after gentle Sister South Wind arrived on the Green Meadows, Peter Rabbit came hopping and skipping down the Lone Little Path from the Green Forest. Peter was happy. He didn't know why. He just was happy. It was in the air. Everybody else seemed happy, too.

Peter had to stop every few minutes just to kick up his heels and try to jump over his own shadow. He had felt just that way ever since gentle Sister South Wind arrived.

> *"I simply have to kick and dance!*
> *I cannot help but gaily prance!*
> *Somehow I feel it in my toes*
> *Whenever gentle South Wind blows."*

So sang Peter Rabbit as he hopped and skipped down the Lone Little Path. Suddenly he stopped right in the middle of the verse. He sat up very straight and stared down at Johnny Chuck's house. Someone was sitting on Johnny Chuck's doorstep. It looked like Johnny Chuck. No,

[20]

it looked like the shadow of Johnny Chuck. Peter rubbed his eyes and looked again. Then he hurried as fast as he could, lipperty-lipperty-lip. The nearer he got, the less like Johnny Chuck looked the one sitting on Johnny Chuck's doorstep. Johnny Chuck had gone to sleep round and fat and roly-poly, so fat he could hardly waddle. This fellow was thin, even thinner than Peter Rabbit himself. He waved a thin hand to Peter.

"Hello, Peter Rabbit! I told you that I would see you in the spring. How did you stand the long winter?"

That certainly was Johnny

"Hello, Peter Rabbit," cried Johnny Chuck

Chuck's voice. Peter was so delighted that in his hurry he fell over his own feet. "Is it really and truly you, Johnny Chuck?" he cried.

"Of course it's me; who did you think it was?" replied Johnny Chuck rather crossly, for Peter was staring at him as if he had never seen him before.

"I—I—I didn't know," confessed Peter Rabbit. "I thought it was you and I thought it wasn't you. What have you been doing to yourself, Johnny Chuck? Your coat looks three sizes too big for you, and when I last saw you it didn't look big enough." Peter hopped all around Johnny Chuck,

[23]

looking at him as if he didn't believe his own eyes.

"Oh, Johnny's all right. He's just been living on his own fat," said another voice. It was Jimmy Skunk who had spoken, and he now stood holding out his hand to Johnny Chuck and grinning good-naturedly. He had come up without either of the others seeing him.

Peter's big eyes opened wider than ever. "Do you mean to say that he has been eating his own fat?" he gasped.

Johnny Chuck and Jimmy Skunk both laughed. "No," said Jimmy Skunk, "he didn't eat it, but he lived on it just the same while he was asleep all winter. Don't you see he hasn't got a particle of fat on him now?"

"But how could he live on it, if he didn't eat it?" asked Peter, staring at Johnny Chuck as if he had never seen him before.

Jimmy Skunk shrugged his shoulders. "Don't ask me. That is one of Old Mother Nature's secrets; you'll have to ask her," he replied.

"And don't ask me," said Johnny Chuck, "for I've been asleep all the time. My, but I'm hungry!"

"So am I!" said another voice. There was Reddy Fox grinning at them. Johnny Chuck dived into the doorway of his house with Peter Rabbit at his heels, for there was nowhere else to go. Jimmy Skunk just stood still and chuckled. He knew that Reddy Fox didn't dare touch him.

III

The Singers of the Smiling Pool

MISTRESS SPRING was making everybody happy on the Green Meadows and in the Green Forest and around the Smiling Pool. With her gentle fingers she wakened one by one all the little sleepers who had spent the long winter dreaming of warm summer days and not knowing anything at all of rough, blustering Brother North Wind or Jack Frost. As they wakened, many began to sing for joy. But the clearest, loudest singers of all lived in the Smiling Pool.

It was a long time before Peter Rabbit and Johnny Chuck knew where they lived. Every night just before going to bed, Johnny Chuck would sit on his doorstep just to listen, and as he listened somehow he felt better and happier; and he always had pleasant dreams after listening to the sweet singers of the Smiling Pool. Even after he had curled himself up for the night deep down in his snug bedroom, he could hear those sweet voices, and whenever he waked up in the night he would hear them.

"Spring! Spring! Spring! Spring!
Beautiful, beautiful, beautiful Spring!
So gentle, so loving, so sweet and so fair!
Oh, who can be cross when there's love in the
air?
Be happy! Be joyful! And join in our song
And help us to send the glad tidings along!
Spring! Spring! Spring! Spring!
Beautiful, beautiful, beautiful Spring!"

When Johnny Chuck had first heard them, he had looked in all the treetops for the singers, but not one could he see. Then he had thought that they must be hidden in the bushes; but when he went to look, he found that the sweet singers were not there. It was very mysterious. Finally he

[*29*]

asked Peter Rabbit if he knew who the sweet singers were and where they were. Peter didn't know, but he was willing to try to find out. Peter is always willing to try to find out about things he doesn't already know about. So Johnny Chuck and Peter Rabbit started out to find the singers.

"I believe they are down in the old bulrushes around the Smiling Pool," said Peter Rabbit, as he stood listening with a hand behind one long ear.

So over to the Smiling Pool they hurried. The nearer they got, the louder became the singing:

"Spring! Spring! Spring! Spring!
Beautiful, beautiful, beautiful Spring!"

But look as they would, they couldn't see a single singer among the brown bulrushes. It was very strange! It seemed as if the voices came right out of the Smiling Pool itself!

When Peter Rabbit made a little noise, as he hopped out on the bank where he could look all over the Smiling Pool, the singing stopped. After he had sat perfectly still for a little while, it began again. There was no doubt about it this time; those voices came right out of the water.

Johnny Chuck stared at Peter Rabbit, and Peter stared at Johnny Chuck. Nobody was to be seen in the Smiling Pool, and yet

They found Jerry Muskrat peeping up at them

there were those voices coming right out of the water.

"How can birds stay under water and still sing?" asked Johnny Chuck.

"Ho, ho, ho! Ha, ha, ha!" Peter Rabbit and Johnny Chuck whirled around, to find Jerry Muskrat peeping up at them from a hole in the bank almost under their feet.

"Ho, ho, ho! That's the best joke this spring!" shouted Jerry Muskrat, and laughed until he had to hold his sides. "Birds under water! Ho, ho, ho!"

IV

Johnny Chuck Finds Out Who the Sweet Singers Are

JOHNNY CHUCK couldn't keep away from the Smiling Pool. No, Sir, Johnny Chuck couldn't keep away from the Smiling Pool. Ever since he and Peter Rabbit had gone over there looking for the sweet singers, who every night and part of the day told all who would listen how glad they were that Mistress Spring had come to the Green Meadows and the Green Forest, Johnny Chuck had had something on his mind. And this is why he couldn't keep away from the Smiling Pool.

You see, it was this way: Johnny and Peter had thought that of course the sweet singers were birds. They hadn't dreamed of anything else. So of course they went looking for birds. When they reached the Smiling Pool, the voices came right out of the water. Johnny knew that some birds, like many of the cousins of Mrs. Quack, can stay under water a long time, and so he didn't know but some other birds might.

Jerry Muskrat was always watching for Johnny, whenever he came to the Smiling Pool, and his eyes would twinkle as he would gravely say:

"Hello, Johnny Chuck! Have you seen the birds sing under water yet?"

Johnny would smile good-naturedly and reply: "Not yet, Jerry Muskrat. Won't you point them out to me?"

Then Jerry would reply:

*"Two eyes you have, bright as can be;
Perhaps some day you'll learn to see."*

Then Johnny Chuck would sit as still as ever he knew how, and watch and watch the Smiling Pool, but not a bird did he see in the water, though the singers were still there. One day a sudden thought popped into his head. Perhaps those singers were not birds at all! Why hadn't he thought of that before? Perhaps it was because he was looking so hard for birds that he hadn't seen anything else. Johnny began to look, not for anything in particular, but to see everything that he could.

Almost right away he saw some tiny little dark spots on the water. They didn't look like much of anything. They were so small that he hadn't noticed them before. One of them was quite close to him, and as Johnny Chuck looked at it, it began to look like a tiny nose, and then—why, just then, Johnny was very sure that one of those singing voices came right from that very spot!

He was so surprised that he hopped to his feet and excitedly beckoned to Jerry Muskrat. The instant he did that, the voices near him stopped singing, and the little spots on the water disappeared, leaving just the tiniest of little rings, just such tiny little rings as drops of rain falling on the Smiling Pool would make. And when that tiny spot nearest to him that looked like a tiny nose disappeared, Johnny Chuck caught just a glimpse of a little form under the water.

"Why—why-e-e! The singers are Grandfather Frog's children!" cried Johnny Chuck.

"No, they're not, but they are own cousins to them; they are the grandchildren of old Mr. Tree Toad and they are called Hylas!" said Jerry Muskrat, laughing and rubbing his hands in great glee. "I told you that if you used your eyes, you'd learn to see."

"My, but they've got voices bigger than they are!" said Johnny Chuck, as he started home across the Green Meadows.

"I'm glad I know who the singers of the Smiling Pool are, and I mustn't forget their name—Hylas. What a funny name!"

But Farmer Brown's boy, listening to their song that evening, didn't call them Hylas. He said: "Hear the peepers! Spring is surely here."

V

Johnny Chuck
Becomes Dissatisfied

JOHNNY CHUCK was unhappy. Here it was the glad spring-time, when everybody is supposed to be the very happiest, and Johnny Chuck was unhappy. Why was he unhappy? Well, he hardly knew himself. He had slept comfortably all the long winter. He had awakened very, very hungry, but now he had plenty to eat. All about him the birds were singing or busily at work building new homes. And still Johnny Chuck felt unhappy. It was dreadful to feel this way and not have any good reason for it.

One bright morning Johnny Chuck sat on his doorstep watching Drummer the Woodpecker building a new home in the old apple tree. Drummer's red head flew back and forth, back and forth, and his sharp bill cut out tiny bits of wood. It was slow work; it was hard work. But Drummer seemed happy, very happy indeed. It was watching Drummer that started Johnny Chuck to thinking about his own home. He had always thought it a very nice home. He had built it just as he wanted it. From the doorstep he could look in all directions over the Green Meadows. It had a front door and a hidden back door. Yes, it was a very nice home indeed.

But now, all of a sudden, Johnny Chuck became dissatisfied with his home. It was too near the Lone Little Path. Too many people knew where it was. It wasn't big enough. The front door ought to face the other way. Dear me, what a surprising lot of faults a discontented heart can find with things that have always been just right! It was so with

Johnny Chuck. That house in which he had spent so many happy days, which had protected him from all harm, of which he had been so proud when he first built it, was now the meanest house in the world. If other people had new houses, why shouldn't he? The more he thought about it, the more dissatisfied and discontented he became and of course the more unhappy. You know one cannot be dissatisfied and discontented and happy at the same time.

Now dissatisfied and discontented people are not at all pleasant to have around. Johnny Chuck had always been one of the best-natured of all the little meadow people, and everybody liked him. So Jimmy Skunk didn't know quite what to make of it, when he came down the Lone Little Path and found Johnny Chuck so out of sorts that he wouldn't even answer when spoken to.

Jimmy Skunk was feeling very good-natured himself. He had just had a fine breakfast of fat beetles and he was at peace with all the world. So he sat down beside Johnny Chuck and began to talk, just as if Johnny Chuck was his usual good-natured self.

"It's a fine day," said Jimmy Skunk.

[45]

Johnny Chuck seemed dissatisfied and discontented

Johnny Chuck just sniffed.

"You're looking very fine," said Jimmy.

Johnny just scowled.

"I think you've got the best place on the Green Meadows for a house," said Jimmy, pretending to admire the view.

Johnny scowled harder than ever.

"And such a splendid house!" said Jimmy. "I wish I had one like it."

"I'm glad you like it! You can have the old thing!" snapped Johnny Chuck.

"What's that?" demanded Jimmy Skunk, opening his eyes very wide.

[47]

"I said that you can have it. I'm going to move," replied Johnny Chuck.

Now he really hadn't thought of moving until that very minute. And he didn't know why he had said it. But he had said it, and because he is an obstinate little fellow he stuck to it.

"When can I move in?" asked Jimmy Skunk, his eyes twinkling.

"Right away, if you want to," replied Johnny Chuck, and swaggered off down the Lone Little Path, leaving Jimmy Skunk to stare after him as if he thought Johnny Chuck had suddenly gone crazy, as indeed he did.

VI

Johnny Chuck Turns Tramp

JOHNNY CHUCK had turned tramp. Yes, Sir, Johnny Chuck had turned tramp. It was a funny thing to do, but he had done it. He didn't know why he had done it, excepting that he had become dissatisfied and discontented and unhappy in his old home. And then, almost without thinking what he was doing, he had told Jimmy Skunk that he he could have the house he had worked so hard to build the summer before and of which he had been so proud. Then Johnny Chuck had swaggered away down the Lone Little Path without once looking back at the home he was leaving.

Where was he going? Well, to tell the truth, Johnny didn't know. He was going to see the world, and perhaps when he had seen the world, he would build him a new house. So as long as he was in sight of Jimmy Skunk, he swaggered along as if he was used to traveling about, without any snug house to go to at night. But down in his heart Johnny Chuck didn't feel half so bold as he pretended.

You see, not since he was a little Chuck and had run away from old Mother Chuck with Peter Rabbit, had he ever been very far from his own doorstep. He had always been content to grow fat and roly-poly right near his own home, and listen to the tales of the great world from Jimmy Skunk and Peter Rabbit and Bobby Coon and Unc' Billy Possum, all of whom are great travelers.

But now, here he was, actually

[51]

setting forth, and without a home to come back to! You see, he had made up his mind that no matter what happened, he wouldn't come back, after having given his house to Jimmy Skunk.

When he had reached a place where he thought Jimmy Skunk couldn't see him, Johnny Chuck turned and looked back, and a queer little feeling seemed to make a lump that filled his throat and choked him. The fact is, Johnny Chuck had already begun to feel homesick. But he swallowed very hard and tried to make himself think that he was having a splendid time. He stopped looking back and started on, and as he tramped along, he tried to sing a song he had once heard Jimmy Skunk sing:

"The world may stretch full far and wide—
What matters that to me?
I'll tramp it up; I'll tramp it down!
For I am bold and free."

It was a very brave little song, but Johnny Chuck didn't feel half so brave and bold as he tried to think he did. Already he was beginning to wonder where he should spend the night. Then he thought of old Whitetail the Marsh Hawk, who had given him such a fright and had so nearly caught him when he was a little fellow. The thought made him look around hastily, and there was old

[53]

Whitetail himself, sailing back and forth hungrily just ahead of him. Fear took possession of Johnny Chuck, and he made himself as flat as possible in the grass, for there was no place to hide. He made up his mind that anyway he would fight.

Nearer and nearer came old Whitetail! Finally he passed right over Johnny Chuck. But he didn't offer to touch him. Indeed, it seemed to Johnny that old Whitetail actually grinned and winked at him. Right then his fear left him.

"Pooh!" said Johnny Chuck scornfully. "Who's afraid of him!" He suddenly realized that he was no longer a helpless little Chuck who couldn't take care of himself, but big and strong, with sharp teeth with which his old enemy had no mind to make a closer acquaintance, when there were mice and snakes to be caught without fighting. So he puffed out his chest and went on, and actually began to enjoy himself, and almost wished for a chance to show how big and strong he was.

VII

Johnny's First Adventure

AFTER old Whitetail the Marsh Hawk passed Johnny Chuck without offering to touch him, Johnny began to feel very brave and bold and important. He strutted and swaggered along as much as his short legs would let him. He held his head very high. Already he felt that he had had an adventure and he longed for more. He forgot the terrible lonesome feeling of a little while before. He forgot that he had given away the only home he had. He didn't know just why, but right down deep inside he had a sudden feeling that he really didn't care a thing about that old home. In fact, he felt as if he wouldn't care if he never had another home. Yes, Sir, that is the way that Johnny Chuck felt. Do you know why? Just because he had just begun to realize how big and strong he really was.

Now it is a splendid thing to feel big and strong and brave, a very splendid thing! But it is a bad thing to let that feeling turn to pride, foolish pride. Of course old Whitetail hadn't really been afraid of Johnny Chuck. He had simply passed Johnny with a wink, because there was plenty to eat without the trouble of fighting, and Whitetail doesn't fight just for the fun of it.

But foolish Johnny Chuck really thought that old Whitetail was afraid of him. The more he thought about it, the more tickled he felt and the more puffed up he felt. He began to talk to himself and to brag. Yes, Sir, Johnny Chuck began to brag:

> *"I'm not afraid of anyone;*
> *They're all afraid of me!*
> *I only have to show my teeth*
> *To make them turn and flee!"*

[58]

"Pooh!" said a voice. "Pooh! It would take two like you to make me run away!"

Johnny Chuck gave a startled jump. There was a strange Chuck glaring at him from behind a little bunch of grass. He was a big, gray old Chuck whom Johnny never had seen on the Green Meadows before, and he didn't look the least bit afraid. No, Sir, he didn't look the teeniest, weeniest bit afraid! Somehow, Johnny Chuck didn't feel half so big and strong and brave as he had a few minutes before. But it wouldn't do to let this stranger know it. Of course not! So, though he felt very small inside, Johnny

[59]

made all his hair bristle up and tried to look very fierce.

"Who are you and what are you doing on my Green Meadows?" he demanded.

"Your Green Meadows! Your Green Meadows! Ho, ho, ho! Your Green Meadows!" The stranger laughed an unpleasant laugh. "How long since you owned the Green Meadows? I have just come down on to them from the Old Pasture, and I like the looks of them so well that I think I will stay. So run along, little boaster! There isn't room for both of us here, and the sooner you trot along the better." The stranger suddenly showed all

his teeth and gritted them un-
pleasantly.

Now when Johnny Chuck heard
this, great anger filled his heart.
A stranger had ordered him to
leave the Green Meadows where
he had been born and always
lived! He could hardly believe
his own ears. He, Johnny Chuck,
would show this stranger who was
master here!

With a squeal of rage, Johnny
sprang at the gray old Chuck.
Then began such a fight as the
Merry Little Breezes of Old
Mother West Wind had never
seen before. They danced around
excitedly and cried: "How dreadful!" and hoped that Johnny

[61]

Johnny sprang at the gray old Chuck

Chuck would win, for you know they loved him very much.

Over and over the two little fighters rolled, biting and scratching and tearing and growling and snarling. Jolly, round, red Mr. Sun hid his face behind a cloud, so as not to see such a dreadful sight. The stranger had been in many fights and he was very crafty. For a while Johnny felt that he was getting the worst of it, and he began to wonder if he really would have to leave the Green Meadows. The very thought filled him with new rage and he fought harder than ever.

Now the stranger was old and his teeth were worn, while

Johnny was young and his teeth were very sharp. After a long, long time, Johnny felt the stranger growing weaker. Johnny fought harder than ever. At last the stranger cried "Enough!" and when he could break away, started back toward the Old Pasture. Johnny Chuck had won!

VIII

Johnny Has Another Adventure

JOHNNY CHUCK lay stretched out on the cool, soft grass of the Green Meadows, panting for breath. He was very tired and very sore. His face was scratched and bitten. His clothes were torn, and he smarted dreadfully in a dozen places. But still Johnny Chuck was happy. When he raised his head to look, he could

see a gray old Chuck limping off
toward the Old Pasture. Once
in a while the gray old Chuck
would turn his head and show
his teeth, but he kept right on
toward the Old Pasture. Johnny
Chuck smiled.

It had been a great fight, and
more than once Johnny Chuck
thought that he should have to
give up. He thought of this now,
and then he thought with shame
of how he had bragged and
boasted just before the fight.
What if he had lost? He resolved
that he would never again brag
or boast. But he also made up
his mind that if anyone should
pick a quarrel with him, he

would show that he wasn't afraid.

It was getting late in the afternoon when Johnny finally felt rested enough to go on. He had got to find a place to spend the night. He hobbled along, for he was very stiff and sore, until he came to the edge of the Green Meadows, where they meet the Green Forest.

Jolly, round, red Mr. Sun was almost ready to go down to his bed behind the Purple Hills. Shadows were already beginning to creep through the Green Forest. Somehow they gave Johnny Chuck that same lonesome feeling that he had had when he first left his old home.

[67]

You see, he had always lived out in the Green Meadows and somehow he was afraid of the Green Forest in the night.

So, instead of going into the Green Forest, he wandered along the edge of it, looking for a place in which to spend the night. At last he came to a hollow log lying just out on the edge of the Green Meadows. Very carefully Johnny Chuck examined it, to be sure that no one else was using it.

"It's just the place I'm looking for!" he said aloud.

Just then there was a sharp hiss, a very fierce hiss. Johnny Chuck felt the hair on his neck

[*68*]

rise as it always did when he heard
that hiss, and he wasn't at all
surprised, when he turned his
head, to find Mr. Blacksnake
close by. Mr. Blacksnake glided
swiftly up to the old log and coiled
himself in front of the opening.
Then he raised his head and ran
out his tongue in the most im-
pudent way.

"Run along, Johnny Chuck!
I've decided to sleep here myself
tonight!" he said sharply.

Now when Johnny Chuck was a
very little fellow, he had been in
great fear of Mr. Blacksnake, as
he had had reason to be. And
because he didn't know any
better, he had been afraid ever

since. Mr. Blacksnake knew this and so now he looked as ugly as he knew how. But you see he didn't know about the great fight that Johnny Chuck had just won.

Now to win an honest fight always makes one feel very strong and very sure of oneself. Johnny looked at Mr. Blacksnake and saw that Mr. Blacksnake didn't look half as big as Johnny had always thought he did. He made up his mind that as he had found the old log first, he had the best right to it.

"I found it first and I'm going to keep it!" snapped Johnny Chuck, and, with every hair on end and gritting his teeth, he

Mr. Blacksnake is a great bluffer

walked straight toward Mr. Black-snake.

Now Mr. Blacksnake is a great bluffer, while at heart he is really a coward. With a fierce hiss he rushed right at Johnny Chuck, expecting to see him turn tail and run. But Johnny stood his ground and showed all his sharp teeth. Instead of attacking Johnny, Mr. Blacksnake glided past him and sneaked away through the grass.

Johnny Chuck chuckled as he crept into the hollow log.

"Only a coward runs away without fighting," he murmured sleepily.

IX

Another Strange Chuck

JOHNNY CHUCK awoke just as jolly, round, red Mr. Sun pulled his own nightcap off. At first Johnny couldn't think where he was. He blinked and blinked. Then he rolled over. "Ouch!" cried Johnny Chuck. You see, he was so stiff and sore from his great fight the day before, that it hurt to roll over. But when he felt the smart of those wounds, he remembered where he was. He was in the old hollow log that he had found on the edge of the Green Meadows just before dark. It was the first time that Johnny had ever slept anywhere excepting underground, and as he lay blinking his eyes, it seemed very strange and rather nice, too.

"Well, well, well! What are you doing here?" cried a sharp voice.

Johnny Chuck looked toward the open end of the old log. There, peeping in, was a little face as sharp as the voice.

"Hello, Chatterer!" cried Johnny.

"I say, what are you doing here?" persisted Chatterer the Red Squirrel, for it was he who was peeking in.

"Just waking up," replied Johnny, with a grin.

"It's time," replied Chatterer. "But that isn't telling me what you are doing so far from home."

"I haven't any home," said Johnny, his face growing just a wee bit wistful.

"You haven't any home!" Chatterer's voice sounded as if he didn't think he had heard aright. "What have you done with it?"

"Given it to Jimmy Skunk," replied Johnny Chuck.

Now Chatterer never gives any-

thing to anybody, and how anyone could give away his home
was more than he could understand. He stared at Johnny as if
he thought Johnny had gone
crazy. Finally he found his
tongue. "I don't believe it!" he
snapped. "If Jimmy Skunk has
got your old home, it's because
he put you out of it."

"No such thing! I'd like to see
Jimmy Skunk or anybody else
put me out of my home!" Johnny
Chuck spoke scornfully. "I gave
it to him because I didn't want
it any longer. I'm going to see
the world, and then I'm going to
build me a new home. Everybody
else seems to be building new

[76]

homes this spring; why shouldn't
I?"

"I'm not!" retorted Chatterer.
"I know enough to know when
I am well off and stay that way.

> *"Who has a discontented heart
> Is sure to play a sorry part."*

Johnny Chuck crawled out of
the old log and stretched himself
somewhat painfully. "That may
be, but there are different kinds
of discontent.

> *"Who never looks for better things
> Will live his life in little rings.*

"Well, I must be moving along,
if I am to see the world."

So Johnny Chuck bade Chatterer good-by and started on. It

Johnny Chuck bade Chatterer good-by

was very delightful to wander over the Green Meadows on such a beautiful spring morning. The violets and the wind-flowers nodded to him, and the dandelions smiled up at him. Johnny almost forgot his torn clothes and the bites and scratches of his great fight with the gray old Chuck the day before. It was fun to just go where he pleased and not have a care in the world.

He was thinking of this as he sat up to look over the Green Meadows. His heart gave a great throb. What was that over near the lone elm tree? It was—yes, it certainly was another Chuck! Could it be the old gray Chuck come back for another fight? A great anger filled the heart of Johnny Chuck, and he whistled sharply. The strange Chuck didn't answer. Johnny ground his teeth and started for the lone elm tree. He would show this other Chuck who was master of the Green Meadows!

X

Why Johnny Chuck Didn't Fight

Anger is an awful thing;
It never stops to reason.
It boils right over all at once,
No matter what the season.

IT WAS SO with Johnny Chuck. The minute he caught sight of the strange Chuck over by the lone elm tree, anger filled his heart and fairly boiled over, until he was in a terrible rage. Of course it was foolish, very foolish indeed. The strange Chuck hadn't said or done anything to make Johnny Chuck angry, not the least thing in the world, excepting to come down on to the Green Meadows. Now the Green Meadows are very broad, and there is room for many Chucks. It was pure selfishness on the part of Johnny Chuck to want to drive away every other Chuck.

But anger never stops to reason. It didn't now. Johnny Chuck hurried as fast as his short legs could take him toward the lone elm tree, and in his mind was just one thought—to drive that strange Chuck off the Green Meadows and to punish him so that he never, never would dare even think of coming back. So great was Johnny's anger that every hair stood on end, and as he ran he chattered and scolded.

"I'll fix him! These are my Green Meadows, and no one else has any business here unless I say so! I'll fix him! I'll fix him!"

Then Johnny would grind his teeth, and in his eyes was the ugliest look. He wasn't nice to see, not a bit nice. The Merry Little Breezes of Old Mother West Wind didn't know what to make of him. Could this be the Johnny Chuck they had known so long, the good-natured, happy Johnny Chuck whom everybody loved? They drew away from

[*83*]

him, for they didn't want anything to do with anyone in such a frightful temper. But Johnny Chuck didn't even notice, and if he had he wouldn't have cared. That is the trouble with anger. It crowds out everything else, when it once fills the heart.

When Johnny had first seen the stranger, he had thought right away that it was the old gray Chuck with whom he had had such a terrible fight the day before and whom he whipped. Perhaps that was one reason for Johnny Chuck's terrible anger now, for the old gray Chuck had tried to drive Johnny Chuck off the Green Meadows.

But when he had to stop for breath and sat up to look again, he saw that it wasn't the old gray Chuck at all. It was a younger Chuck and much smaller than the old gray Chuck. It was smaller than Johnny himself.

"He'll be all the easier to whip," muttered Johnny, as he started on again, never once thinking of how unfair it would be to fight with one smaller than himself. That was because he was so angry. Anger never is fair.

Pretty soon he reached the lone elm tree. The stranger wasn't to be seen! No, Sir, the stranger wasn't anywhere in sight. Johnny Chuck sat up and looked this way and looked that way, but the stranger was nowhere in sight.

"Pooh!" said Johnny Chuck. "He's afraid to fight! He's a coward. But he can't get away from me so easily. He's hiding, and I'll find him and then—" Johnny didn't finish, but he ground his teeth, and it wasn't a pleasant sound to hear.

So Johnny Chuck hunted for the stranger, and the longer he hunted the angrier he grew. Somehow the stranger managed to keep out of his sight. He was almost ready to give up, when he almost stumbled over the stranger, hiding in a little clump of

"I'm Polly Chuck," replied the stranger

bushes. And then a funny thing happened. What do you think it was?

Why, all the anger left Johnny Chuck. His hair no longer stood on end. He didn't know why, but all of a sudden he felt foolish, very foolish indeed.

"Who are you?" he demanded gruffly.

"I—I'm Polly Chuck," replied the stranger, in a small, timid voice.

XI

The Greatest Thing in the World

JOHNNY CHUCK had begun to think about his clothes. Yes, Sir, he spent a whole lot of time thinking about how he looked and wishing that he had a handsomer coat. For the first time in all his life he began to envy Reddy Fox, because of the beautiful red coat of which Reddy is so proud. It seemed to Johnny that his own coat was so plain and so dull that no one would look at it twice. Besides, it was torn now, because of the great fight Johnny had had with the old gray Chuck who came down from the Old Pasture. Johnny smoothed it down and brushed it carefully and tried to make himself look as spick and span as he knew how.

"Oh, dear!" he sighed. "I don't see why Old Mother Nature didn't give me as handsome a coat as she did Reddy Fox. And there are Jimmy Skunk and Happy Jack the Gray Squirrel

[90]

and—and—why, almost everyone has a handsomer coat than I have!"

Now this wasn't at all like Johnny Chuck. First he had been discontented with his house and had given it to Jimmy Skunk. Now he was discontented with his clothes. What was coming over Johnny Chuck? He really didn't know himself. At least, he wouldn't have admitted that he knew. But right down deep in his heart was a great desire —the desire to have Polly Chuck admire him. Yes, Sir, that is what it was! And it seemed to him that she would admire him a great deal more if he wore fine clothes. You see, he hadn't learned yet what Peter Rabbit had learned a long time ago, which is that

Fine clothes but catch the passing eye;
Fine deeds win love from low and high.

So Johnny Chuck wished and wished that he had a handsome suit, but as he didn't, and no amount of wishing would bring him one, he made the one he did have look as good as he could, and then went in search of Polly Chuck.

Sometimes she would not notice him at all. Sometimes he would find her shyly peeping at him from behind a clump of grass. Then Johnny Chuck would try to make himself look very important, and would strut about as if he really did own the Green Meadows.

Sometimes she would hide from him, and when he found her she would run away. Other times she would be just as nice to him as she could be, and they would have a jolly time hunting for sweet clover and other nice things to eat. Then Johnny Chuck's heart would swell until it seemed to him that it would fairly burst with happiness.

Instead of wanting to drive Polly Chuck away from the Green Meadows, as he had the old gray Chuck, Johnny began to worry

[93]

for fear that Polly Chuck might not stay on the Green Meadows. Whenever he thought of that, his heart would sink way, way down, and he would hurry to look for her and make sure that she was still there.

When he was beside her, he felt very big and strong and brave, and longed for a chance to show her how brave he was. She was such a timid little thing herself that the least little thing frightened her, and Johnny Chuck was glad that this was so, for it gave him a chance to protect her.

When he wasn't with her, he spent his time looking for new patches of sweet clover to take her to. At first she wouldn't go without a great deal of coaxing, but after a while he didn't have to coax at all. She seemed to delight to be with him as much as he did to be with her.

So Johnny Chuck grew happier and happier. He was happier than he had ever been in all his life before. You see, Johnny Chuck had found the greatest thing in the world. Do you know what it is? It is called love.

XII

Johnny Chuck
Proves His Love

THESE SPRING DAYS were beautiful days on the Green Meadows. It seemed to Johnny Chuck that the Green Meadows never had been so lovely or the songs of the birds so sweet. He had forgotten all about his old friends, Jimmy Skunk and Peter Rabbit and the other little meadow people.

You see, he couldn't think of

anybody but Polly Chuck, and he didn't want to be with anybody but Polly Chuck. He had even forgotten that he had started out to see the world. He didn't care anything more about the world. All he wanted was to be where Polly Chuck was. Then he was perfectly happy. That was because Johnny Chuck had found the greatest thing in the world, which is love. But Johnny still had one great wish, the wish that he might show Polly Chuck just how brave and strong he was and how well he could take care of her.

One morning they were feasting in a patch of sweet clover over near an old stone wall. It was the same stone wall in which Johnny Chuck had escaped from old Whitetail the Marsh Hawk, when Johnny was a very little fellow.

Suddenly Polly gave a little scream of fright. Johnny Chuck looked up to see a dog almost upon her. Johnny's first thought was to run to the old stone wall. He was nearer to it than Polly was. Then he saw that that dreadful dog would catch Polly before she could reach the stone wall.

A great rage filled Johnny's heart, just as it had when he had fought the old gray Chuck. Every hair stood on end, not with fear, but with anger, and he sprang in front of Polly.

"Run, Polly, run!" he cried, and Polly ran.

But Johnny didn't run. Oh, my, no! Johnny didn't run. He drew himself together ready to spring. He showed all his sharp teeth and ground them savagely. Little sparks of fire seemed to snap out of his eyes. There was no sign of fear in Johnny Chuck then, not the least little bit. Just in front of him the dog stopped and barked. He was a little dog, a young and foolish dog, and he was terribly excited. He barked until he almost lost his breath. He didn't like the looks of

[*99*]

Johnny Chuck's sharp teeth. So he circled around Johnny, trying to get behind him. But Johnny turned as the dog circled, and always the little dog found those sharp teeth directly in front of him. He barked and barked, until it seemed as if he would bark his head off.

Finally the little dog, who was young and foolish, grew tired of just dancing around and barking. "Pooh!" said he to himself. "He's nothing but a Chuck!" Then he stopped barking and sprang straight at Johnny with an ugly growl.

Johnny Chuck was ready for him and he was quicker than the

[100]

little dog. His sharp teeth closed on one of the little dog's ears, and he held on while with his stout claws he scratched and tore.

The little dog, who was young and foolish and hadn't yet learned how to fight, couldn't get hold of Johnny Chuck anywhere. Then he tried to shake Johnny Chuck off, but he couldn't, because Johnny held on to that ear with his sharp teeth.

"Kiyi-yi-yi-yi!" yelled the little dog, for those teeth hurt dreadfully. "Kiyi-yi-yi-yi!"

Over and over they rolled and tumbled, the little dog trying to get away, and Johnny Chuck holding on to the little dog's ear.

[101]

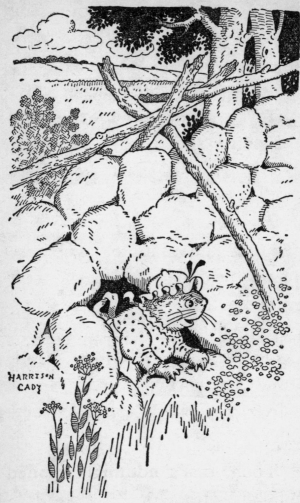

Johnny found Polly peeping out at him

Finally Johnny had to let go to get his breath. The little dog sprang to his feet and started for home across the Green Meadows as fast as he could run.

Johnny Chuck shook himself and grinned, as he heard the little dog's "Kiyi-yi-yi" grow fainter and fainter. "I'm glad it wasn't Bowser the Hound," muttered Johnny Chuck, as he started toward the old stone wall. There he found Polly Chuck peeping out at him, and all of a tremble with fright.

"My, how brave you are!" said Polly Chuck.

"Pooh, that's nothing!" replied Johnny Chuck.

XIII

Polly and Johnny Chuck Go House Hunting

J OHNNY CHUCK was happy. Yes, Sir, Johnny Chuck was happy —so happy that he felt like doing foolish things. You see, Johnny Chuck loved Polly Chuck and he knew now that Polly Chuck loved him. He had known it ever since he had fought with the foolish little dog who had dared to frighten Polly Chuck.

After the fight was over, and the little dog had been sent home kiyi-yi-ing, Polly Chuck had crept out of the old stone wall where she had been hiding and snuggled up beside Johnny Chuck and looked at him as if she thought him the most wonderful Chuck in all the world, as, indeed, she did. And Johnny had felt his heart swell and swell with happiness until it almost choked him.

So now once more Johnny Chuck began to think of a new home. He had forgotten all about seeing the world. All he wanted now was a new house, built just so, with a front door and a hidden back door, and big enough for two, for no more would Johnny Chuck live alone. So, with shy little Polly Chuck by his side, he began to search for a place to make a new home.

The more he thought about it, the more Johnny wanted to build his house over by the lone elm tree where he had first seen Polly Chuck. It was a splendid place. From it you could see a great way in every direction. It would be shady on hot summer days. It was near a great big patch of sweet clover. It seemed to Johnny

Chuck that it was the best place on all the Green Meadows. He whispered as much to Polly Chuck. She turned up her nose.

"It's too low!" said she.

"Oh!" replied Johnny, and looked puzzled, for really it was one of the highest places on the Green Meadows.

"Yes," said Polly, in a brisk, decided way, "it's altogether too low. Probably it is wet."

"Oh!" said Johnny once more. Of course he knew that it wasn't wet, but if Polly didn't want to live there, he wouldn't say a word. Of course not.

"Now there's a place right over there," continued Polly. "I think we'll build our house right there."

Johnny opened his mouth to say something, but he closed it again without speaking and meekly trotted after Polly Chuck to the place she had picked out. It was in a little hollow. Johnny knew before he began to dig that the ground was damp, almost wet. But if Polly wanted to live there she should, and Johnny began to dig. By and by he stopped to rest. Where was Polly? He looked this way and that way anxiously. Just as he was getting ready to go hunt for her, she came hurrying back.

"I've found a perfectly lovely

place for our new home!" she cried.

Johnny looked ruefully at the hole he had worked so hard to dig; then he brushed the dirt from his clothes and followed her. This time Johnny had no fault to find with the ground. It was high and dry. But Polly had chosen a spot close to a road that wound down across the Green Meadows. Johnny shook his head doubtfully, but he began to dig. This time, however, he kept one eye on Polly Chuck, and the minute he found that she was wandering off, he stopped digging and chuckled as he watched her. It wasn't long before back she came in great excitement. She had found a better place!

So they wandered over the Green Meadows, Polly leading the way. Johnny had learned by this time to waste no time digging. And he had made up his mind to one thing. What do you think it was? It was this: He would follow Polly until she found a place to suit him, but when she did find such a place she shouldn't have a chance to change her mind again.

XIV

A New Home at Last

Home, no matter where it be,
Or it be big or small,
Is just the one place in the world
That dearest is of all.

JOHNNY CHUCK was thinking of
this as he worked with might
and main. It was a new house
that he was building, but already
he felt that it was home, and
every time he thought of it he
felt a queer little tugging at his
heart. You see, while it was his

[*111*]

Johnny was building a new house

home, it was Polly Chuck's home, too, and that made it doubly dear to Johnny Chuck, even before it was finished.

And where do you think Johnny was building his new home? It was clear way over on the edge of Farmer Brown's old orchard! Yes, Sir, after all the fuss Johnny Chuck had made over any other Chuck living on the Green Meadows, and after driving the old gray Chuck back to the Old Pasture, Johnny Chuck had left the Green Meadows himself!

It wasn't of his own accord that Johnny Chuck had left the Green Meadows. No, indeed! He loved them too well for that. But he loved Polly Chuck more, and although he had grumbled a little, he had followed her up to the old orchard, and now they were going to stay there. Sometimes Johnny shivered when he thought how near were Farmer Brown and Farmer Brown's boy and Bowser the Hound.

He had never been so far from his old home on the Green Meadows before, and it was all very strange up here. It was very lovely, too. Besides, it was in this very old orchard that Polly Chuck had been born, and she knew every part of it. Johnny felt better when he found that out. So he set to work to build a home, and this time he meant business. Polly Chuck could change her mind as many times as she pleased; that was going to be their home and that was where they were going to live.

Now Johnny Chuck had grown wise in the ways of the world since he first ran away from the home where he was born. Twice since then he had built a new home, and now this would be better than either of the others. He paid no heed to Polly, when she pouted because he did not dig where she wanted him to. He went from tree to tree, big old apple trees they were, and at

[115]

the very last tree, way down in a corner near a tumbled-down stone wall, he found what he wanted— two spreading roots gave him a chance to dig between them.

Polly watched him get ready for work and she pouted some more.

"It would be a lot nicer out in that grassy place, and a lot easier to dig," said she.

Johnny Chuck smiled and made the dirt fly. "It certainly would be easier to dig," said he, when he stopped for breath, "easier for me and easier for Bowser the Hound or for old Granny Fox, if either wanted to dig us out. Now, these old roots are just far enough apart for us to go in and out. They make a beautiful doorway. But Bowser the Hound cannot get through if he tries, and he can't make our doorway any larger. Don't you see how safe it is?"

Polly Chuck had to own up that it was safer than a home in the open could possibly be, and Johnny went on digging. He made a long hall down to the snuggest of bedrooms, deep, deep down underground. Then he made a long back hall, and all the sand from this he carried out the front way. By and by he made a back door at the end of the back hall, and it opened right behind a big stone fallen from the old stone wall. You would never have guessed that there was a back door there.

His new house was finished now, and Johnny Chuck and Polly Chuck sat on the doorstep and watched jolly, round, red Mr. Sun go to bed behind the Purple Hills and were happy.

XV

Sammy Jay Finds the New Home

JOHNNY CHUCK was missed from his old home on the Green Meadows. If he had known how much he was missed, he certainly would have tried to go back for at least a call on his old neighbors. There had been great surprise when it had been discovered that Jimmy Skunk was living in Johnny's old house, and at first some of the little meadow people were inclined to look at Jimmy a wee bit distrustfully when he told how Johnny Chuck had given away his house.

When Johnny sent back word by the Merry Little Breezes that it was true, they believed Jimmy Skunk and forgot the unpleasant things that they had begun to hint at about him. But they one and all thought that Johnny Chuck must be crazy. Yes, Sir, they thought that Johnny Chuck must be crazy. They were sure of it when the Merry Little Breezes brought word of how Johnny had started out to see the world.

But everybody was so busy

about their own affairs in the beautiful bright springtime that they couldn't spend much time wondering about Johnny Chuck. They missed him every time they passed his old house and then forgot him; that is, most of the little meadow people did.

Peter Rabbit didn't.

Peter used to stop every day to gossip with Johnny Chuck and tell him all the news, and now that Johnny Chuck was no longer there, Peter missed him greatly. Jimmy Skunk was always asleep or off somewhere. Besides, he was such a traveler that he knew all the news almost as soon as Peter himself.

The Merry Little Breezes told
Peter that Johnny Chuck was still
on the Green Meadows, hunting
for a new home, so Peter made
up his mind that just as soon as
Johnny got settled, Peter would
hunt him up and call. You see,
he never dreamed that Johnny
would leave the Green Meadows,
and he thought that of course the
Merry Little Breezes would tell
him just where Johnny Chuck's
new house was, whenever it was
built. But there is where Peter
made a mistake.

The Merry Little Breezes are
the friends of all the little
meadow and forest people, but
they wouldn't be very long if

they told everything that they
find out.

Their merry tongues they guard full well
And things they shouldn't ever tell,
For long ago they learned the way
To keep a secret night and day.

And so when they found
Johnny Chuck's new house in the
corner of Farmer Brown's old
orchard, they promised Johnny
that they wouldn't tell anybody,
and they didn't. So it was a long
time before anyone else found
out what had become of Johnny
Chuck, for no one thought of
looking in the corner of the old
orchard.

The Merry Little Breezes used
to come every day and bring

Johnny Chuck the news, and he and Polly Chuck would laugh and tickle, as they thought of Peter Rabbit hunting and hunting and never finding them.

Then one morning, as Johnny Chuck sat on his doorstep, half dozing in the sun with his heart filled with contentment, he happened to look up straight into two sharp eyes peering down at him from among the leaves of the apple tree under which he had built his house. He knew those eyes. They were such sharp eyes that they were unpleasant. He didn't even have to look for the blue and white coat of the owner to know who had found his snug home. But he pretended to keep right on dozing, and pretty soon the owner of the eyes disappeared without making a sound.

"Oh dear me," sighed Johnny Chuck, "now the whole world will know where we live, for that was Sammy Jay." Then his face brightened as he added: "Anyway, he didn't see Polly Chuck, and he doesn't know anything about her, so I'll keep twice as sharp a watch as before."

XVI

Sammy Jay Plans Mischief

Mischief may not mean to be really truly bad,
But somehow it seems to make other people sad;
Does a mean unpleasant thing and tries to think
*   it fun;*
Then, alas, it runs away when trouble has
*   begun.*

OF ALL the little people who live in the Green Forest and on the Green Meadows, none is more mischievous than Sammy Jay. It seems sometimes as if there was more mischief under that pert little cap Sammy Jay wears than in the heads of all the other little meadow and forest people put together. When he isn't actually in mischief, Sammy Jay is planning mischief. You see, it has grown to be a habit with Sammy Jay, and habits, especially bad habits, have a way of growing and growing.

Now Sammy Jay had no quarrel with Johnny Chuck. Oh, my, no! He would have told you that he liked Johnny Chuck. Everybody likes Johnny Chuck. But just as soon as Sammy Jay found Johnny Chuck's new house, he began to plan mischief. He didn't really want any harm to come to

[*127*]

Johnny Chuck, but he wanted to make Johnny uncomfortable. That is Sammy Jay's idea of fun—seeing somebody else uncomfortable. So he slipped away to a thick hemlock tree in the Green Forest to try to think of some plan to tease Johnny Chuck and make him uncomfortable.

Of course he knew that Johnny had hidden his new house in the corner of Farmer Brown's old orchard because he wanted it to be a secret. He didn't know why Johnny wanted it a secret and he didn't care. If Johnny wanted it a secret, it would be fun to tell everybody about it. As he sat wondering whom he should tell first, he saw Reddy Fox trotting down the Lone Little Path.

"Hi, Reddy Fox!" he shouted.

Reddy looked up. "Hello, Sammy Jay! What have you got on your mind this morning?" said Reddy.

"Nothing much," replied Sammy. "What's the news?"

Reddy grinned. "There isn't any news," said he. "I was just going to ask you the same thing."

It was Sammy Jay's turn to grin. "Just as if I could tell you any news, Reddy Fox! Just as if I could tell you any news!" he exclaimed. "Why, everybody knows that you are so smart that

[129]

you find out everything as soon as it happens."

Reddy Fox felt flattered. You know people who do a great deal of flattering themselves are often the very easiest to flatter if you know how. Reddy pretended to be very modest, but no one likes to be thought smart and important more than Reddy Fox does, and it pleased him greatly that Sammy Jay should think him so smart that no one could tell him any news. Sammy knew this perfectly well, and he chuckled to himself as he watched Reddy Fox pretending to be so modest.

"Have you called on Johnny Chuck at his new home yet?"

"Have you called on Johnny Chuck yet?"
asked Sammy Jay

asked Sammy Jay, in the most matter-of-fact way.

"No," replied Reddy, "but I mean to, soon." He said this just as if he knew all about Johnny Chuck's new home, when all the time he hadn't the remotest idea in the world where it was. In fact, he had hunted and hunted for it, but hadn't found a trace of it. And all the time Sammy Jay knew that Reddy didn't know where it was. But Sammy didn't let on that he knew.

"I just happened to be up in Farmer Brown's old orchard this morning, so I thought I'd pay Johnny Chuck a call," said Sammy, and chuckled as he saw

Reddy's ears prick up. "By the way, he thinks you don't know where he lives now."

"Huh!" said Reddy Fox. "As if Johnny Chuck could fool me! Well, I must be moving along. Good-by, Sammy Jay."

Reddy trotted off toward the Green Meadows, but the minute he was out of sight of Sammy Jay, he turned toward Farmer Brown's old orchard, just as Sammy Jay had known he would.

"I guess Johnny Chuck will have a visitor," chuckled Sammy Jay, as he started to look for Jimmy Skunk.

XVII

More Mischief

Mischief's like a snowball
Sent rolling down a hill;
With every turn it bigger grows
And bigger, bigger still.

SAMMY JAY had started mischief
by telling Reddy Fox where
Johnny Chuck's new house was.
If you had asked him, Sammy Jay
would have said that he hadn't
told. All he had said was that
he had happened to be up in

Farmer Brown's old orchard and so had called on Johnny Chuck in his new house.

Now Reddy Fox is very sly, oh, very sly. He had pretended to Sammy Jay that he knew all the time where Johnny Chuck was living. When he left Sammy Jay, he had started in the direction of the Green Meadows, just as if he had no thought of going over to Farmer Brown's old orchard.

But Sammy Jay is just as sly as Reddy Fox. He wasn't fooled for one minute, not one little minute. He chuckled to himself as he started to look for Jimmy Skunk. Then he changed his mind.

"I think I'll go up to the old

orchard myself!" said Sammy Jay, and away he flew.

He got there first and hid in the top of a big apple tree, where he could see all that went on. It wasn't long before he saw Reddy Fox steal out from the Green Forest and over to the old orchard. Reddy was nervous, very nervous. You see, it was broad daylight, and the old orchard was very near Farmer Brown's house. Reddy knew that he ought to have waited until night, but he knew that then Johnny Chuck would be fast asleep. Now, perhaps, Johnny Chuck, thinking that no one knew where he lived, would not be on watch, and so he might be able to catch Johnny.

So Reddy, with one eye on Farmer Brown's house and one eye on the watch for some sign of Johnny Chuck, stole into the old orchard. Every few steps he would stop and look and listen. At every little noise he would start nervously. Then Sammy Jay would chuckle under his breath.

So Reddy Fox crept and tip-toed about through the old orchard. Every minute he grew more nerv-ous, and every minute he grew more disappointed, for he could find no sign of Johnny Chuck's house. He began to think that Sammy Jay had fooled him, and the very thought made him grind his teeth. At last he decided to give it up.

He was down in the far corner of the old orchard, close by the old stone wall now, and he got all ready to jump over the old stone wall, when he just happened to look on the other side of the big apple tree he was under, and there was what he was looking for—Johnny Chuck's new house! Johnny Chuck wasn't in sight, but there was the new house, and Johnny must be either inside or not far away. Reddy grinned. It was a sly, wicked, hungry grin. He flattened himself out in the grass behind the big apple tree.

"I'll give Johnny Chuck the surprise of his life!" muttered Reddy Fox under his breath.

Now Sammy Jay had been watching all this time. He knew that Johnny Chuck was safely inside his house, for Johnny had seen Reddy when he first came into the old orchard. And Sammy knew that Johnny Chuck knew that when Reddy found that new house, he would hide just as he had done.

"Johnny Chuck won't come out again today, and there won't be any excitement at all," thought Sammy Jay in disappointment, for he had hoped to see a fight between Reddy Fox and Johnny

Chuck. Just then Sammy looked over to Farmer Brown's house, and there was Farmer Brown's boy getting ready to saw wood. The imp of mischief under Sammy's pert cap gave him an idea. He flew over to the old apple tree, just over Reddy's head, and began to scream at the top of his lungs.

Farmer Brown's boy stopped work and looked over toward the old orchard.

"When a Jay screams like that there is usually a Fox around," he muttered, as he unfastened Bowser the Hound.

XVIII

Farmer Brown's Boy Makes a Discovery

REDDY FOX glared up at Sammy Jay. "What's the matter with you?" snarled Reddy Fox. "Why don't you mind your own affairs, instead of making trouble for other people?" You see, Reddy was afraid that Johnny Chuck would hear Sammy Jay and take warning.

"Hello, Reddy Fox! I thought you had gone down to the Green

Meadows!" Sammy said this as if he was very much surprised to see Reddy there. He wasn't, for you know he had been watching Reddy hunt for Johnny Chuck's new house, but Reddy had pretended that he was going down to the Green Meadows early that morning, and so now Sammy pretended that he had thought that Reddy really had gone.

"I changed my mind!" he snapped. "What are you screaming so for?"

"Just to exercise my lungs, so as to be sure that I can scream when I want to," replied Sammy, screaming still louder.

"Well, go somewhere else and

[142]

scream; I want to sleep," said Reddy crossly.

Now Sammy Jay knew perfectly well that Reddy Fox had no thought of taking a nap but was hiding there to try to catch Johnny Chuck. And Sammy knew that Farmer Brown's boy could hear him scream, and that he knew that when Sammy screamed that way it meant there was a Fox about. Sitting in the top of the apple tree, Sammy could see Farmer Brown's boy starting for the old orchard, with Bowser the Hound running ahead of him.

Farmer Brown's boy had no gun, so Sammy knew that no harm would come to Reddy, but

[143]

that Reddy would get a dreadful scare; and that is what Sammy wanted, just out of pure mischief. So he screamed louder than ever.

Reddy Fox lost his temper. He sat up and called Sammy Jay all the bad names he could think of. He forgot where he was. He told Sammy Jay what he thought of him and what he would do to him if he ever caught him.

Sammy Jay kept right on screaming. He made such a noise that Reddy didn't hear footsteps coming nearer and nearer. Suddenly there was a great roar right behind him. "Bow, wow, wow! Bow, wow, wow, wow!"—just like that.

Reddy was so frightened that he didn't even look to see where he was jumping, and bumped his head against the apple tree. Then he started for the Green Forest, with Bowser the Hound at his heels.

Sammy Jay laughed till he lost his breath and nearly tumbled off his perch. Then he flew away, still laughing. He thought it the greatest joke ever.

Farmer Brown's boy had followed Bowser the Hound into the old orchard.

"I wonder what a Fox was doing up here in broad daylight," said he, talking to himself. "Perhaps one of my hens has

*Reddy started for the Green Forest with Bowser
at his heels*

stolen her nest down here, and he has found it. I'll have a look, anyway."

So he walked on down to the far corner of the old orchard, straight to the place from which he had seen Reddy Fox jump. When he got there, of course he saw Johnny Chuck's new house right away.

"Ho!" cried Farmer Brown's boy. "Brer Fox was hunting Chucks. I'll keep my eye on this, and if Mr. Chuck makes any trouble in my garden, I'll know where to catch him."

XIX

Johnny Chuck's Pride

EVER SINCE Farmer Brown's boy and Reddy Fox had found his new house in the far corner of the old orchard, Johnny Chuck had been worried. It was not that he was afraid for himself. Oh, my, no! Johnny Chuck felt perfectly able to take care of himself. But there was Polly Chuck! He was terribly afraid that something might happen to Polly Chuck.

[*148*]

You see, she was not big and strong like him, and then Polly Chuck was apt to be careless. So for a while Johnny Chuck worried a great deal.

But Reddy Fox didn't come again in daytime. You see, Bowser the Hound had given him such a scare that he didn't dare to. He sometimes came at night and sniffed hungrily at Johnny Chuck's doorway, but Johnny and Polly were safe inside, and this didn't trouble them a bit. And Farmer Brown's boy seemed to have forgotten all about the new house. So after a while Johnny Chuck stopped worrying so much. The fact is Johnny Chuck had

[149]

something else to think about. He had a secret. Yes, Sir, Johnny Chuck had a secret, and he kept it well.

Sammy Jay came up to the old orchard almost every morning. His sharp eyes were not long in finding out that Johnny Chuck had a secret, but try as he would he could not find out what that secret was. Whatever it was, it made Johnny Chuck very happy. He would come out on his door-step and smile and sometimes give a funny little whistle of pure joy.

It puzzled Sammy Jay a great deal. He couldn't see why Johnny Chuck should be any happier than he ever was. To be sure it was a happy time of year. Everybody was happy, for it was springtime, and the Green Forest and the Green Meadows, even the Old Pasture, were very lovely. But somehow Sammy Jay felt that it was something more than this, a secret that Johnny Chuck was keeping all to himself, that was making him so happy. But what it was, Sammy Jay couldn't imagine. He spent so much time thinking about it and wondering what it could be, that it actually kept him out of mischief.

One morning Johnny Chuck came out, looking happier than ever. He chuckled and chuckled as only a happy Chuck can. Then he did foolish things. He kicked up his heels. He rolled over and over in the grass. He whistled. He even tried to sing, which is something no Chuck can do or should ever try to do. Then suddenly he scrambled to his feet, carefully brushed his coat, and tried to look very dignified. He strutted back and forth in front of his doorway, as if he was very proud of something. There was pride in the very way in which he took each step. There was pride in the very way in which he held his head. It was too much for Sammy Jay.

"What are you so proud about,

Johnny Chuck?" he demanded, in his harsh voice. "If I didn't have a better-looking coat than you've got, I wouldn't put on airs!"

You know Sammy Jay is very proud of his own handsome blue and white coat and dearly loves to show it off.

"It isn't that," said Johnny Chuck.

"Well, if it is because you think yourself so smart to hide yourself up here in the old orchard, let me tell you that I found you out long ago, and so did Reddy Fox, and Bowser the Hound, and Farmer Brown's boy," sneered Sammy Jay in the most disagreeable way.

"It isn't that," said Johnny Chuck.

"Well, what is it, then?" snapped Sammy Jay.

"That's for you to find out," replied Johnny Chuck.

"There's foolish pride and silly pride and pride of low degree;
A better pride is honest pride, and that's the pride for me."

With that, Johnny Chuck disappeared in his new house.

XX

Sammy Jay
Understands

IT WAS a beautiful morning.
Jolly, round, red Mr. Sun had
thrown his bedclothes off very
early and started to climb up the
sky, smiling his broadest. Old
Mother West Wind had swept
his path clear of clouds. The
Merry Little Breezes, who, you
know, are Mother West Wind's
children, had danced across the
Green Meadows up to the old

orchard, where they pelted each other with white and pink petals of apple blossoms until the ground was covered. Each apple tree was like a huge bouquet of loveliness. Yes, indeed, it was very beautiful that spring morning.

Sammy Jay had gotten up almost as early as Mr. Sun and Old Mother West Wind. As soon as he had swallowed his breakfast, he flew up to the old orchard and hid among the white and pink apple blossoms to watch for Johnny Chuck. You see, he knew that Johnny Chuck had some sort of a secret which filled Johnny with very great pride; but what it was Sammy Jay couldn't even

[*156*]

guess, and nothing troubles Sammy Jay quite so much as the feeling that he cannot find out the secrets of other people. So he sat very, very still among the apple blossoms and waited and watched.

By and by Johnny Chuck appeared on his doorstep. He seemed very much excited, did Johnny Chuck. He sat up very straight and looked this way and looked that way. He looked up in the apple trees, and Sammy Jay held his breath, for fear that Johnny would see him. But Sammy was so well hidden that, bright as Johnny Chuck's eyes are, they failed to see him. Then

Johnny Chuck actually climbed up on the old stone wall so as to see better, and he sat there a long time, looking and looking.

Sammy Jay grew impatient. "He seems to be terribly watchful this morning. I never knew him to be so watchful before. I don't understand it," muttered Sammy to himself.

After a while Johnny Chuck seemed quite satisfied that there was no one about. He hopped down from the old stone wall and scampered over to the doorway of his new house, and there he began to chatter. Sammy Jay stretched his neck until it ached, trying to hear what Johnny Chuck was saying, but he couldn't because Johnny's head was inside his doorway.

Pretty soon Johnny Chuck backed out and sat up, and he looked very proud and important. Then Sammy Jay saw something that nearly took his breath away. It was the head of Polly Chuck peeping out of the doorway. It was the first time that he had seen Polly Chuck.

"Why," gasped Sammy Jay, "it must be that Johnny Chuck has a mate, and I didn't know a thing about it! So that's his secret and the reason he has appeared so proud lately!"

Polly Chuck came out on the

doorstep. She looked just as proud as Johnny Chuck, and at the same time she seemed terribly anxious. She sat up beside Johnny Chuck, and she looked this way and that way, just as Johnny had. Then she put her head in at the doorway and began to call in the softest voice.

In a minute Sammy Jay saw something more. It surprised him so that he nearly lost his balance. It was another head peeping out of the doorway, a head just like Johnny Chuck's, only it was a teeny, weeny one. Then there was another and another! Polly kept talking and talking in the softest voice, while Johnny Chuck

Johnny knew that his secret was a secret no longer

swelled himself up until he looked as if he would burst with pride.

Sammy Jay understood now why Johnny Chuck had been so proud for the last few days. It was because he had a family! Sammy looked down at the three little Chucks sitting on the door-step, trying to sit up the way Johnny Chuck sat, and they looked so funny that Sammy forgot himself and laughed right out loud. In a flash the three little Chucks and Polly Chuck had disappeared inside the house, while Johnny Chuck looked up angrily. He knew that his secret was a secret no longer.

[162]

XXI

Sammy Jay Has a Change of Heart

There's no one ever quite so bad
That somewhere way down deep inside
A little goodness does not find
A place wherein to creep and hide.

IT IS SO with Sammy Jay. Yes, Sir, it is so with Sammy Jay. You may think that because Sammy Jay is vain, a troublemaker and a thief, he is all bad. He isn't. There is some good in Sammy Jay, just as there is some good in everybody. If there wasn't,

[*163*]

Old Mother Nature never, never would allow Sammy Jay to go his mischievous way through the Green Forest. He dearly loves to get other people into all kinds of trouble, and this is one reason why nobody loves him. But if you watch out sharp enough, you will find that hidden under that beautiful blue and white coat of his there really is some good. You may have to look a long time for it, but sooner or later you will find it. Johnny Chuck did.

Sammy Jay had already made a lot of trouble for Johnny Chuck. You see, he had been the first of the little forest and meadow people to find Johnny Chuck's new house. And then, just to make trouble for Johnny Chuck, he had told Reddy Fox about it, and after that he had called Bowser the Hound and Farmer Brown's boy over to it. Now he had discovered Johnny Chuck's greatest secret—that Johnny had a family. What a chance to make trouble now!

Sammy started for the Green Forest as fast as his wings could take him. He would tell Reddy Fox and Redtail the Hawk. They were very fond of young Chucks. It would be great fun to see the fright of Johnny Chuck and his family when Reddy Fox or Redtail the Hawk appeared.

Sammy Jay chuckled wickedly as he flew. When he reached the Green Forest and stopped in his favorite hemlock tree to rest, he was still chuckling. But by that time it was a different kind of a chuckle. Yes, Sir, it was a different kind of a chuckle. It was a better chuckle to hear. The fact is, Sammy Jay was no longer chuckling over the thought of the trouble he could make. He was laughing at the memory of how funny those three little baby Chucks had looked sitting up on Johnny Chuck's doorstep and trying to do whatever Johnny Chuck did. The more he thought about it, the more he tickled and laughed.

Right in the midst of his laughter along came Redtail the Hawk. Sammy Jay opened his mouth to call to Redtail and tell him about Johnny Chuck's secret. Then he closed it again with a snap.

"I won't tell him yet," said Sammy to himself, "for he might catch one of those baby Chucks, and they are such funny little fellows that that would really be too bad. I guess I'll wait awhile." And with that, off flew Sammy Jay to hunt for some other mischief. You see, he had had a change of heart. The little goodness way down deep inside had come out of hiding.

[*167*]

But of course Johnny Chuck didn't know this, and over in his new house in the far corner of the old orchard, he and Polly Chuck were worrying and worrying, for they felt sure that now everyone would know their secret, and it wouldn't be safe for the dear little baby Chucks to so much as put their funny little noses outside the door.

XXII

Johnny Chuck
Is Kept Busy

JOHNNY CHUCK is naturally lazy. You see, Johnny has very simple tastes and usually he is contented. He does not have to go far from his own doorstep to get all he wants to eat. He does not have to hunt for his food, as so many of the little meadow and forest people do, and so he has a great deal of time to sit on his doorstep and watch the world go by and dream pleasant daydreams and grow fat. Now people who do not have to work usually become lazy. It is the easiest habit in the world to learn and the hardest to get over. And so, because he seldom has to work, Johnny Chuck quite naturally is lazy.

But Johnny can work when there really is need of it. No one, unless it is Digger the Badger or Miner the Mole, can dig faster than Johnny Chuck. And when there is real need of working, Johnny works with a will. When he was a very tiny Chuck, old

[*170*]

Mother Chuck had taught him
this:

"When work there is that must be done
Don't fret and whine and spoil the day!
The quicker that you do your work
The longer time you'll have to play."

Johnny never has forgotten this,
and when it is really necessary
that he should work, no one
works harder than he does. But
he always first makes sure that it
is necessary work and that he will
not be wasting his time in doing
foolish, unnecessary things.

And now Johnny Chuck was
the busiest he had ever been in
all his life. If he felt lazy these
beautiful spring days, he didn't
have time to think about it. No,

[*171*]

Sir, he actually didn't have time to remember that he is naturally lazy. You see, he had a family to look out for—three babies to find sweet, tender young clover for and to teach all the things that every Chuck should know, and to watch out for, that no harm should come to them. So Johnny Chuck was busy, so busy that he hardly had time to eat enough.

Every morning Johnny would come out as soon as jolly, round, red Mr. Sun began his daily climb up in the blue, blue sky. He would look this way and look that way to make sure that Reddy Fox or Granny Fox or Redtail the Hawk or Bowser the

Hound or any other danger was nowhere near. And he never forgot to look up in the apple trees to make sure that Sammy Jay was not there. Then he would call to Polly Chuck and the three baby Chucks.

Polly Chuck would come out with a very worried air, and after her would come the three funny little baby Chucks, who would roll and tumble over each other on the doorstep. When he thought they had played enough, Johnny Chuck would lead the way along a little private path which he had made through the grass. After him, one behind another, would trot the three

[*173*]

little Chucks, and behind them would march Polly Chuck, to see that none went astray.

When they reached the patch of tender, sweet young clover, Johnny Chuck would sit up very straight and still, watching as sharp as he knew how for the least sign of danger. When the three little stomachs were full of sweet, tender young clover, he would proudly lead the way home again, and then as before he would sit up very straight and watch for danger, while the three baby Chucks sprawled out on the doorstep for a sun nap.

Oh, those were busy days for Johnny Chuck, and anxious days, too! You see, he had not forgotten that Sammy Jay had found out his secret, and he hadn't the least doubt in the world that Sammy Jay would tell Reddy Fox. So, from the first thing in the morning until the very last thing at night, Johnny Chuck was on the watch for danger.

And all the time, though Johnny didn't know it, a pair of sharp eyes were watching him from a snug hiding place in one of the old apple trees. Whose were they? Why, Sammy Jay's, to be sure. You see, Sammy Jay hadn't told Johnny Chuck's great secret, after all.

XXIII

The School in the Old Orchard

Little Foxes, little Chucks,
  Little Squirrels, Mice and Mink,
Just like little boys and girls,
  Go to school to learn to think.

YOU DIDN'T KNOW that, did
you? Well, it's a fact. Yes, Sir,
it's a fact. All the babies born
in the Green Forest or on the
Green Meadows or around the
Smiling Pool have to go to school
just as soon as they are big
enough to leave their own door-

[*176*]

steps. They go to the greatest school in the world, and it is called the School of Experience.

Old Mother Nature has charge of it, but the teachers usually are father and mother for the first few weeks, anyway. After that Old Mother Nature herself gives them a few lessons, and a very stern teacher she is. They just have to learn her lessons. If they don't, something dreadful is almost sure to happen.

Of course Sammy Jay knew all this, because he had had to go to school when he was a little fellow. So Sammy was not much surprised when, from his snug hiding place in one of the old apple trees, he discovered that there was a school in Farmer Brown's old orchard. Johnny Chuck was the teacher and his three baby Chucks were the pupils. Sammy Jay was so interested in that funny little school in the old orchard that he quite forgot to think about mischief.

The very first lesson that the three little Chucks had to learn was obedience. Johnny Chuck was very particular about that. You see, he knew that unless they learned this first of all, none of the other lessons would do them much good. They must first learn to mind instantly, without asking questions. Dear me, dear me,

Johnny Chuck certainly did have his hands full, teaching those three little Chucks to mind! They were such lively little chaps, and there was so much that was new and wonderful to see, that it was dreadfully hard work to sit perfectly still, just because Johnny Chuck told them to. But if they didn't mind instantly, they were sure to have their ears soundly boxed, and sometimes were sent back to the house without a taste of the sweet, tender young clover of which they were so fond.

After a few lessons of this kind, they found out that it was always best to obey instantly, and

[179]

then Johnny began to teach them other things, things which it is very important that every Chuck should know.

First, there were signals. When Johnny whistled a certain way, it meant "A stranger in sight; possible danger!"

Then each little Chuck would sit up very straight and not move the teeniest, weeniest bit, so that from a little distance they looked for all the world like tiny stumps. But all the time their sharp little eyes would be looking this way and that way, to see what the danger might be. After a while Johnny would give another little whistle, which meant

"Danger past." Then they would once more begin to fill their little stomachs with sweet, tender young clover.

Sometimes, however, Johnny would whistle sharply. That meant "Run!" Then they would scamper as fast as they could along the nearest little path to the house under the old apple tree in the far corner, and never once look around. They would dive head first, one after the other, in at the doorway, and not show their noses outside again until Johnny or Polly Chuck told them they could.

Then there was a still different whistle. It meant "Danger very

[*181*]

near; lie low!" When they heard that, they flattened themselves right down in the grass just wherever they happened to be, and held their breath and didn't move until Johnny signaled that they might. Of course, there never was any real danger. Johnny was just teaching them, so that when danger did come, as it surely would, sooner or later, they would know just what to do.

It surely was a funny little school, and sometimes Sammy Jay had hard work to keep from laughing right out.

XXIV

Sammy Jay Proves That He Is Not All Bad

SAMMY JAY hadn't had so much fun for a long time as he found in watching the funny little school in Farmer Brown's old orchard, where Johnny Chuck was teaching his three baby Chucks the things that every little Chuck must learn, if he would grow up into a big Chuck.

Sammy Jay watched Johnny teaching
his three baby Chucks

When they had learned to mind without waiting to ask why, and had learned the signals which told them just what to do when danger was near, Johnny began to lead them farther and farther away from home.

He took them up along the old stone wall and showed them how to find safe hiding places among the stones. Then he took them off a little way and suddenly gave the danger signal. It was funny, very funny indeed, to see the three little Chucks scamper for the old stone wall and crawl out of sight.

The first time, two of them tried to squeeze into the same

hole together, and each was in such a hurry that he wouldn't let the other go first. Then both lost their tempers and they began to fight about it, quite forgetting that if there was really any danger near, they surely would come to harm. Such a scolding as Johnny Chuck did give those two little Chucks! Then he made them try it all over again.

Once he found a footprint which Reddy Fox had made in some soft earth during the night, and made each little Chuck smell of it, while he told them all about Reddy and old Granny Fox and how smart and sly they were and how very, very fond they

were of tender young Chucks for
dinner.

The three little Chucks shivered when they smelled of Reddy's track, and the hair along
their backs stood up in a way
that was very funny to see.

Then Johnny Chuck took
them over to the edge of the
old orchard, where they could
peep out over the Green Meadows. He pointed out old Whitetail the Marsh Hawk, sailing back
and forth over the meadows, and
told them how once, when he
was a little Chuck and had run
away from home, old Whitetail
had nearly caught him. He told
them about Farmer Brown's boy

and about Bowser the Hound and a great many other things that little Chucks should learn about.

Now all the time that Johnny Chuck was teaching these things, he was keeping the sharpest kind of a watch for danger, and there were many times when he would give the danger signal. Then they would all lie flat down in the grass and keep perfectly still, or else scamper as fast as they could along the little paths which Johnny had made, to the safety of the snug home under the old apple tree. But even the most watchful are surprised sometimes.

One morning, when Johnny

Chuck had led the three little Chucks farther from home than usual, Farmer Brown's boy took it into his head to visit the old orchard. Johnny Chuck did not see him coming. You see, the orchard grass had grown so tall that even when he sat up his very straightest, Johnny could not always see over the top of it. So this morning he failed to see Farmer Brown's boy coming.

But Sammy Jay, sitting in his snug hiding place in the top of one of the old apple trees, saw him. At first Sammy Jay's sharp eyes twinkled. There would be some fun now! Perhaps Farmer Brown's boy would catch one of the little Chucks! Sammy Jay could picture to himself the fright of Johnny Chuck and the three little Chucks. He fairly hugged himself in delight, for you know Sammy Jay dearly loves to see other people in trouble.

Then he thought of all the fun he had had watching those three little Chucks learn their lessons, and suddenly the thought of anything happening to them made Sammy Jay feel uncomfortable. Almost without stopping to think, he screamed at the top of his lungs:

"Run, Johnny Chuck, run! Here comes Farmer Brown's boy!"

And Johnny Chuck ran. He didn't wait to ask questions or even to look. He started the three little Chucks ahead of him, and he nipped their heels to make them run faster. And just in time they reached the snug house under the old apple tree in the far corner.

Farmer Brown's boy was just in time to see them disappear. He watched Sammy Jay flying over to the Green Forest and screaming "Thief! thief!" as he flew.

"I wonder now if that Jay warned those Chucks purposely," said he, as he scratched his head thoughtfully.